Geronimo Stilton
ENGLISH!

3 MY BODY 我的身體

新雅文化事業有限公司
www.sunya.com.hk

Geronimo Stilton English
MY BODY 我的身體

作　　者：Geronimo Stilton 謝利連摩・史提頓
譯　　者：Phoebe Wong
責任編輯：王燕參
封面繪圖：Giuseppe Facciotto
插圖繪畫：Claudio Cernuschi, Andrea Denegri, Daria Cerchi
內文設計：Angela Ficarelli, Raffaella Picozzi
出　　版：新雅文化事業有限公司
　　　　　香港筲箕灣耀興道3號東匯廣場9樓
　　　　　營銷部電話：（852）2562 0161
　　　　　客戶服務部電話：（852）2976 6559
　　　　　傳真：（852）2597 4003
　　　　　網址：http://www.sunya.com.hk
　　　　　電郵：marketing@sunya.com.hk
發　　行：香港聯合書刊物流有限公司
　　　　　香港新界大埔汀麗路36號中華商務印刷大廈3字樓
　　　　　電話：（852）2150 2100　傳真：（852）2407 3062
　　　　　電郵：info@suplogistics.com.hk
印　　刷：C & C Offset Printing Co.,Ltd
　　　　　香港新界大埔汀麗路36號
版　　次：二〇一一年二月初版
　　　　　10 9 8 7 6 5 4 3 2 1

CONTENTS
目錄

BENJAMIN'S CLASSMATES 班哲文的老師和同學們   4

GERONIMO AND HIS FRIENDS 謝利連摩和他的家鼠朋友們   5

HI! 你好！   6
    A SONG FOR YOU! - What's Your Name?

MY FACE 我的臉   8

MY FACE, YOUR FACE 我的臉，你的臉   10
    A SONG FOR YOU! - My Face, Your Face

MY HAIR 我的頭髮   12

I AM, I'M 我是   14

YOU ARE, YOU'RE 你是   15
    A SONG FOR YOU! - We Are Good Friends

MY BODY 我的身體   16
    A SONG FOR YOU! - Body, My Body Rap

TURN RIGHT, TURN LEFT 向右轉，向左轉   18
    A SONG FOR YOU! - Clap Your Hands!

A TIRING DAY 令人疲倦的一天   20

TEST 小測驗   24

DICTIONARY 詞典   25

GERONIMO'S ISLAND 老鼠島地圖   30

EXERCISE BOOK 練習冊

ANSWERS 答案

BENJAMIN'S CLASSMATES
班哲文的老師和同學們

Maestra Topitilla
托比蒂拉‧德‧托比莉斯

Rarin
拉琳

Diego
迪哥

Rupa
露芭

Tui
杜爾

David
大衛

Sakura
櫻花

Mohamed
穆哈麥德

Tian Kai
田凱

Oliver
奧利佛

Milenko
米蘭哥

Trippo
特里普

Carmen
卡敏

Atina
阿提娜

Esmeralda
愛絲梅拉達

Pandora
潘朵拉

Takeshi
北野

Kuti
菊花

Benjamin
班哲文

Hsing
阿星

Laura
羅拉

Kiku
奇哥

Antonia
安東妮婭

Liza
麗莎

GERONIMO AND HIS FRIENDS
謝利連摩和他的家鼠朋友們

謝利連摩・史提頓 Geronimo Stilton
一個古怪的傢伙，簡直可以說是一隻笨拙的文化鼠。他是《鼠民公報》的總裁，正花盡心思改變報紙業的歷史。

菲・史提頓 Tea Stilton
謝利連摩的妹妹，她是《鼠民公報》的特派記者，同時也是一個運動愛好者。

班哲文・史提頓 Benjamin Stilton
謝利連摩的小侄兒，常被叔叔稱作「我的小乳酪」，是一隻感情豐富的小老鼠。

潘朵拉・華之鼠 Pandora Woz
柏蒂・活力鼠的小侄女、班哲文最好的朋友，是一隻活潑開朗的小老鼠。

柏蒂・活力鼠 Patty Spring
美麗迷人的電視新聞工作者，致力於她熱愛的電視事業。

賴皮 Trappola
謝利連摩的表弟，非常喜歡食物，風趣幽默，是一隻饞嘴、愛開玩笑的老鼠，善於將歡樂傳遞給每一隻鼠。

麗萍姑媽 Zia Lippa
謝利連摩的姑媽，對鼠十分友善，又和藹可親，只想將最好的給身邊的鼠。

艾拿 Iena
謝利連摩的好朋友，充滿活力，熱愛各項運動，他希望能把對運動的熱誠傳給謝利連摩。

史奎克・愛管閒事鼠 Ficcanaso Squitt
謝利連摩的好朋友，是一個非常有頭腦的私家偵探，總是穿着一件黃色的乾濕樓。

HI! 你好！

親愛的小朋友，很高興和你一起開始新的學習。這次，我們會學習如何用英語說出我們身體各部分的名稱，我們還會一起唱歌，一起跳舞……不用擔心，相信你自己一定能做得到！首先讓我們以一種新的、你不知道的方式來互相打招呼。很快，你就能學會如何用英語說出你的名字了！準備好了嗎？讓我們開始吧！

⭐ 你能回答菲的問題嗎？試着用英語說出你的名字。

A SONG FOR YOU!

Track 1

What's Your Name?

What's your name?
What's your name?
I'm Benjamin! I'm Benjamin!
What's your name?
What's your name?
Please, tell me,
what's your name?

❗ **What's your name?**
你叫什麼名字?

跟我謝利連摩·史提頓一起學英文,
就像玩遊戲一樣簡單好玩!

你可以一邊看着圖畫一邊讀。
以下有幾個標誌,你要特別留意:

🧀 當看到 💿 標誌時,你可以聽CD,
一邊聽,一邊跟着朗讀,還可以跟
着一起唱歌。

🧀 當看到 ⭐ 標誌時,你可以和朋友
們一起玩遊戲,或者嘗試回答問
題。題目很簡單,它們對鞏固你所
學過的內容很有幫助。

🧀 當看到 ❗ 標誌時,你要注意看一
下格子裏的生字,反覆唸幾遍,掌
握發音。

最後,不要忘記完成小測驗和練習
冊裏的問題!看看你有多聰明吧。

祝大家學得開開心心!

謝利連摩·史提頓

答案:你回答時應該唱出「Hi, I'm」作開頭。
例如:Hi, I'm Benjamin.

MY FACE 我的臉

　　放學後，班哲文和潘朵拉常常來我家，一起做功課。今天，潘朵拉做完功課後，向我請教有關臉上各部分的英文名稱。我正在用英語教他們說呢，head（頭），face（臉），eye（眼睛），ear（耳朵），nose（鼻子），mouth（嘴巴），tongue（舌頭），cheek（臉頰）和 tooth（牙齒），潘朵拉和班哲文一起重複說着這些生字，你也跟着一起說說看。

head　　　　face　　　　eye　　　　ear　　　　nose

mouth　　　tongue　　　cheek　　　tooth

講解完畢之後，我讓潘朵拉和班哲文趕快開始練習。潘朵拉卻跑到鏡子前，一邊對着鏡子做動作，一邊用英語說出身體各部分的名稱，班哲文也在一旁做着各種滑稽的表情。你也跟着他們一起一邊做動作，一邊說說看吧。

指着你的眼睛説
my eye!

搔搔你的耳朵説
my ear!

張開你的嘴巴説
my mouth!

伸出你的舌頭説
my tongue!

撓撓你的頭説
my head!

擦擦你的臉説
my face!

捏捏你的臉頰説
my cheek!

碰碰你的牙齒説
my tooth!

看着你的鼻尖説
my nose!

| tooth | 牙齒 |
| teeth | tooth 的眾數 |

9

MY FACE, YOUR FACE
我的臉，你的臉

　　班哲文和潘朵拉不停地做着各種滑稽的表情，大家都忍不住大笑起來。這時，潘朵拉想到一個好主意：他們可以一邊玩遊戲一邊學習。他們請我幫忙播放音樂，然後跟着一起唱歌。當歌聲響起時，歌詞唱到什麼，他們就做出和歌曲內容相關的動作，並且用英語說出聽到的內容。你也想試試嗎？和他們一起唱吧！

your face...

A SONG FOR YOU!
Track 2

My Face, Your Face
My face, your face
my face, your face.
My face, your face
my mouth, your mouth
my tongue, your tongue
my nose, your nose.
My head, your head
my cheeks, your cheeks
my ears, your ears
my eyes, your eyes.
My face, your face!
My face, your face
my face, your face.
My face, your face
my mouth, your mouth
my tongue, your tongue
my nose, your nose.
My teeth, your teeth
my ears, your ears
my eyes, your eyes
your beautiful eyes!

your mouth...

 your
你的 / 你們的

your tongue...

 10

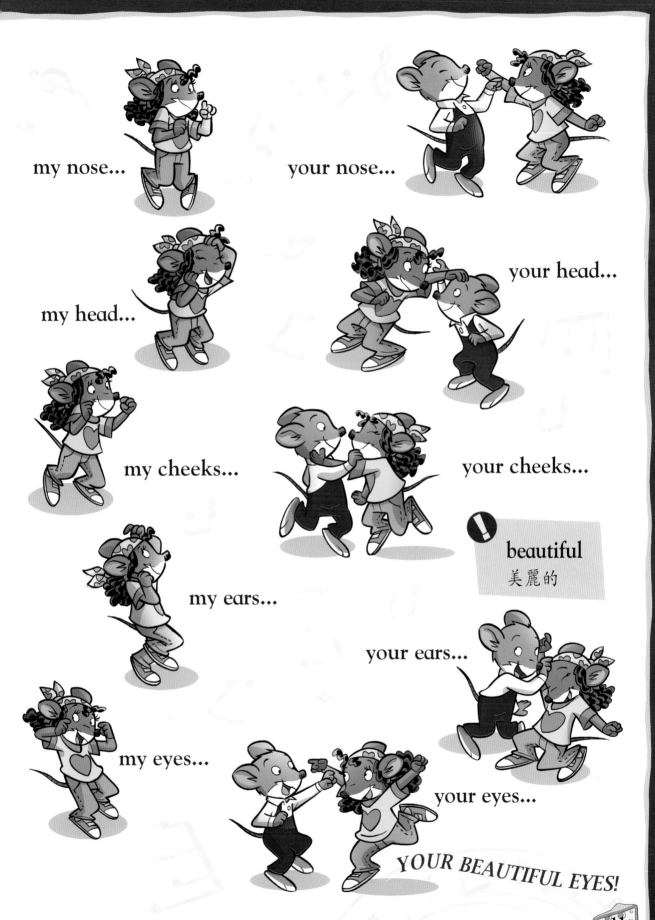

my nose...

your nose...

my head...

your head...

my cheeks...

your cheeks...

beautiful
美麗的

my ears...

your ears...

my eyes...

your eyes...

YOUR BEAUTIFUL EYES!

11

MY HAIR 我的頭髮

這天放學後，班哲文和潘朵拉神神秘秘地向我家走來。一陣悅耳的門鈴聲響起，會是誰呢？我趕緊去開門，一陣男孩女孩的嘈吵聲馬上傳進耳朵，原來是班哲文和潘朵拉，還有他們的同班同學們。潘朵拉想邀請我和他們一起玩遊戲：每個人都要說出自己的頭髮是什麼顏色或什麼髮型，你也跟着一起說說看。

black hair	黑色的頭髮
blonde hair	金黃色的頭髮
brown hair	棕色的頭髮
red hair	紅色的頭髮
curly hair	曲髮
straight hair	直髮
long hair	長髮
short hair	短髮

My hair is black.

My hair is brown.

My hair is blonde.

My hair is red.

My hair is long.

My hair is straight.

My hair is short.

my hair is
我的頭髮是

ponytail	馬尾辮
plaits	辮子
very	很 / 非常
nice	好看

My hair is curly.

My hair is short and curly.

My hair is long and straight.

Look at my ponytail.

Look at my plaits.

Very nice!

⭐ 你的頭髮是什麼顏色的？髮型是怎樣的？
試着用英語描述一下你的頭髮。

My hair is ...

。著曲或著直、著長、著短或著短是以可也，色顏的髮頭你出說以可你：示提

13

I AM, I'M 我是

　　班哲文、潘朵拉和他們的同學一起度過了一個愉快的、充滿歡笑的下午。他們非常投入地玩遊戲，誰也沒有注意到班哲文已經悄悄地走開了。當他回來時，所有的同學都發出一陣哈哈的大笑聲。為什麼呢？原來班哲文偷偷穿上了我的衣服！他說……

I'm Stilton. Geronimo Stilton.

No, I am Geronimo Stilton. You are Benjamin Stilton.

I am / I'm
我是
you are / you're
你是

YOU ARE, YOU'RE 你是

我以一千塊莫澤雷勒乳酪發誓，現在我們就缺一首歌助興！於是班哲文和潘朵拉即興地唱了一首歌給同學們聽。我以乳酪擔保，他們真的很了不起，你也來和他們一起唱吧。

A SONG FOR YOU! Track 3

We Are Good Friends

I'm Benjamin, you're Pandora.

I'm Pandora, you're Benjamin.

I'm a boy, you're a girl.

I'm a girl, you're a boy, a pretty boy!

I'm a good boy, you're a good girl!

WE ARE GOOD FRIENDS!!!

we are
我們是

boy	男孩	a good boy	一個好男孩
girl	女孩	a good girl	一個好女孩
friends	朋友	good friends	好朋友
good	好	a pretty boy	一個漂亮的男孩
		a pretty girl	一個漂亮的女孩

MY BODY 我的身體

班哲文邀請我和他們一起唱歌，可是我一點也不想唱，因為我感到很害羞。最後，我還是經不起班哲文的再三請求，所以決定唱一首歌。不過，在唱歌之前，我希望小朋友能先學會用英語說出身體各部分的名稱：身體、手臂、手、腿、腳和尾巴……你也和他們一起大聲讀出來吧！

body
my body

body	身體
arm	手臂
arms	arm 的眾數
hand	手
hands	hand 的眾數
leg	腿
legs	leg 的眾數
foot	腳
feet	foot 的眾數
tail	尾巴

arm
my arms
hand
my hands

everybody	每個人
look at me	看着我
repeat	重複
me	我

Body, My Body Rap

Everybody look at me
and repeat with me!
Body!
My body!

Arm!
My arms!
Hand!
My hands!

Leg!
My legs!
Foot...
my feet!
And your tail?
Oh, yes, my tail!

my legs

leg

foot

my feet

And your tail?

Oh, yes, my tail.

17

TURN RIGHT, TURN LEFT
向右轉，向左轉

當大家跟着我唱完歌後，便輪到菲表演跳舞了。班哲文和他的同學們在一旁看着，不一會兒，他們就情不自禁地加入了菲的行列，和她一起跳起舞來。他們隨着音樂，一邊說出動作的名稱，一邊跳，這真是一次很特別的跳舞課呀！你還不來試一下？一起來吧！

① Clap your hands!

② Stamp your feet!

③ Walk!

④ Turn right!

⑨ Turn left!

⑧ And... walk!

⑩ Turn right!

clap	拍手
stamp	踩腳
walk	走路
sit	坐下
stand up	起立

18

5 Turn left!

6 And... sit down!

7 Now... stand up!

Clap Your Hands!

Hello, everybody!
Now, let's dance together!
Clap your hands!
Stamp your feet!
Walk! Walk! Walk!
Turn right! Turn left!
And sit down!

Now... stand up!
And... walk!
Turn left! Turn right!
Stamp your feet!
Turn left! Turn right!
Clap your hands!
Clap your hands!
Clap your hands!

11 Stamp your feet!

12 Clap your hands!

〈令人疲倦的一天〉

潘朵拉和班哲文要去上學了，但他們想先跟謝利連摩說再見。

班哲文：你好，謝利連摩叔叔！

謝利連摩：你好！

菲：你們今天有沒有會令人疲倦的課呀？

潘朵拉：我們有體育課。

謝利連摩：那一定是讓人非常疲倦的課！

20

菲：上體育課是很有趣的啊！
謝利連摩：上體育課簡直是糟透了！

菲：再見，孩子們，好好享受你們的上課時間吧！
謝利連摩：再見，一會兒見！
班哲文、潘朵拉：再見！

菲：你也應該去做做運動，這對你有好處！
謝利連摩：但是，我已經做了很多運動啦……

謝利連摩：特別是我的手指！

菲：好，但是……

菲：你需要全身運動啊！

Tea convinces Geronimo to go with her to the Topgym.

Hello, Mr. Stilton! How about some weights today?

菲說服了謝利連摩和她一起去健身室。

教練：你好，史提頓先生！今天練練啞鈴好嗎？

Yes, but... I have brought my own weights!

謝利連摩：好的，不過……我帶了自己的啞鈴來！

One... two...three...four... Geronimo can lift the weights, but...

一……二……三……四……謝利連摩舉起了那些啞鈴，但是……

His personal trainer looks at them closely and...

他的私人教練定眼地看着那些啞鈴……

These are balloons! Mr. Stilton, that's not fair!

教練：這些都是氣球來的！史提頓先生，這樣很不誠實！

教練：史提頓先生，首先做做熱身，來，跟我一起做。
謝利連摩：哎喲！我的手臂很痛！

教練：現在輪到壓腿！
謝利連摩：哎喲！我的腿很痛！

謝利連摩開始跑步，但是他跌倒了！
謝利連摩：哎喲！我的頭很痛！

教練：史提頓先生，你真是無藥可救了！
菲：來吧，我們回家去吧！

The End

回家後，在廚房裏……

謝利連摩：看，這才是我最喜歡的運動！
菲：那是你嘴巴、牙齒和舌頭的運動！

TEST 小測驗

⭐ 1. 你能用英語說出下面身體各部分的名稱嗎？說說看。

| 頭 | 臉 | 眼睛 | 鼻子 | 嘴 |

| 舌頭 | 牙齒 | 耳朵 | 臉頰 | 頭髮 |

⭐ 2. 你會用英語說出自己的名字嗎？試着說一說。

My name's ...　　　　　　**I'm ...**

⭐ 3. 用英語說出下面的短語。

(a) 我的手臂　　　(b) 我的身體　　　(c) 我的手

(d) 我的腳　　　(e) 我的腿

⭐ 4. 用英語說出下面的句子。

(a) 我的頭髮是金黃色的。
My... is...

(b) 我的頭髮是黑色的。
My... is...

(c) 我的頭髮是長的。
My... is...

(d) 我的頭髮是短的。
My... is...

DICTIONARY 詞典

（英、粵、普發聲）

A

and　和

arm　手臂

B

balloon　氣球

beautiful　美麗的

black　黑色

blonde　金黃色

body　身體

boy　男孩

brown　棕色

C

cheek　臉頰

clap　拍手

convince　説服

curly　鬈曲的

D

dance　跳舞

do　做

E

ear　耳朵

enjoy　享受

especially　特別

everybody　每個人

exercise　運動

eye　眼睛

F

face　臉

fair　誠實

fall　跌倒

favourite　最喜歡的

feet　腳（foot的眾數）

finger　手指

first　首先

follow　跟着

foot　腳

friend　朋友

fun　有趣的

G

girl　女孩

go　去

good　好

goodbye　再見

H

hair　頭髮

hand　手

have　有

head　頭

hello　你好

K

kid　孩子

kitchen　廚房

L

left　左

leg　腿

lift　舉起

long　長的

look at me　看着我

M

me　我

mouth　嘴巴

my　我的

N

name　名字

nice　好看

nose　鼻子

now　現在

P

personal　私人

physical education　體育

plaits　辮子

please　請

ponytail　馬尾辮

pretty　漂亮的

R

red　紅色

repeat　重複

right　右

run　跑

S

say　說

school　學校

see you later　一會兒見

short　短的

sit down　坐下

stamp　踩腳

stand up　起立

straight　直的

T

tail　尾巴

teeth　牙齒（tooth的眾數）

tell me　告訴我

terrible　糟透了

tiring　疲倦的

today　今天

together　一起

tongue　舌頭

tooth　牙齒

trainer　教練

turn　轉動

27

V

very 　很／非常

W

walk 　走路
want 　想
we 　我們

Y

you 　你／你們
your 　你的／你們的

看在一千塊莫澤雷勒乳酪的份上，你學得開心嗎？很開心，對不對？好極了！跟你一起跳舞唱歌我也很開心！我等着你下次繼續跟班哲文和潘朵拉一起玩一起學英語呀。現在要說再見了，當然是用英語說啦！

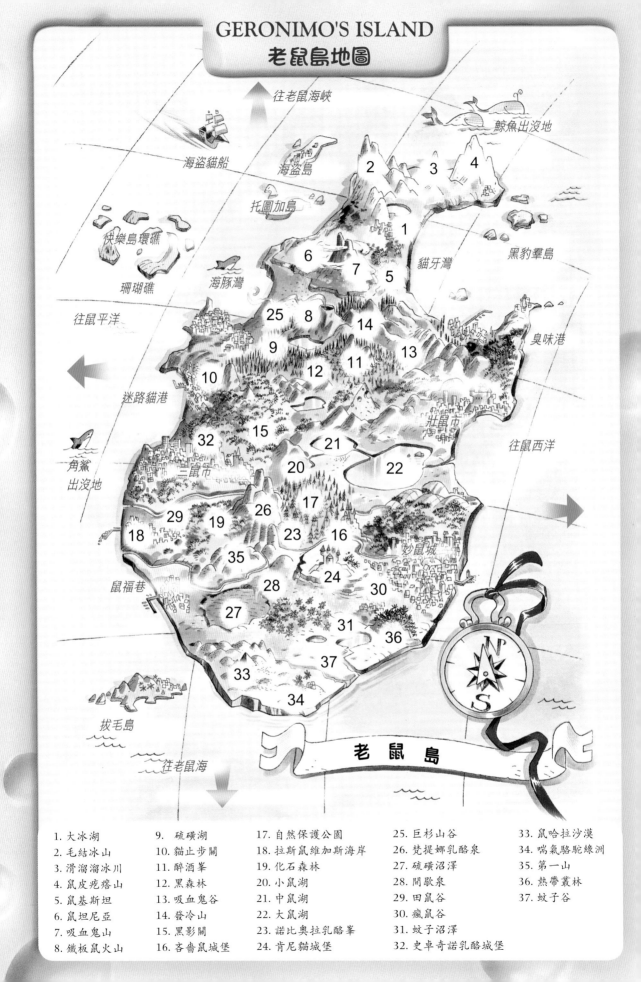

GERONIMO'S ISLAND
老鼠島地圖

往老鼠海峽

鯨魚出沒地

海盜貓船　海盜島

托圖加島

快樂島環礁

珊瑚礁　海豚灣

往鼠平洋

迷路貓港

角鯊
出沒地

貓牙灣

黑豹羣島

臭味港

壯鼠市

往鼠西洋

三鼠市

妙鼠城

鼠福巷

拔毛島

往老鼠海

老 鼠 島

1. 大冰湖
2. 毛結冰山
3. 滑溜溜冰川
4. 鼠皮疙瘩山
5. 鼠基斯坦
6. 鼠坦尼亞
7. 吸血鬼山
8. 鐵板鼠火山
9. 硫磺湖
10. 貓止步關
11. 醉酒峯
12. 黑森林
13. 吸血鬼谷
14. 發冷山
15. 黑影關
16. 客魯鼠城堡
17. 自然保護公園
18. 拉斯鼠維加斯海岸
19. 化石森林
20. 小鼠湖
21. 中鼠湖
22. 大鼠湖
23. 諾比奧拉乳酪峯
24. 肯尼貓城堡
25. 巨杉山谷
26. 梵提娜乳酪泉
27. 硫磺沼澤
28. 間歇泉
29. 田鼠谷
30. 瘋鼠谷
31. 蚊子沼澤
32. 史卓奇諾乳酪城堡
33. 鼠哈拉沙漠
34. 喘氣駱駝綠洲
35. 第一山
36. 熱帶叢林
37. 蚊子谷

Geronimo Stilton

EXERCISE BOOK

練習冊

想知道自己對 MY BODY 掌握了多少，
趕快打開後面的練習完成它吧！

ENGLISH!

3 **MY BODY** 我的身體

MY FACE, YOUR FACE
我的臉，你的臉

⭐ 根據各老鼠的話，在他們臉上相應的部位填上顏色。

MY BODY, YOUR BODY
我的身體，你的身體

⭐ 根據下面的句子，在圖中圈出正確的身體部位。

1. Circle my body.

2. Circle my right arm.

3. Circle my left arm.

4. Circle my left hand.

5. Circle my right leg.

6. Circle my right foot.

7. Circle my left foot.

8. Circle my feet.

9. Circle my hands.

10. Circle my arms.

MY HAIR, YOUR HAIR
我的頭髮，你的頭髮

⭐ 根據各老鼠的話，把他們的頭髮填上適當的顏色，然後在橫線上填充。

1. *My hair is red.*

your＿＿＿＿＿hair

2. *My hair is brown.*

your＿＿＿＿＿hair

3. *My hair is black.*

your black＿＿＿＿＿

4. *My hair is blonde.*

your＿＿＿＿＿hair

5.

My hair is long and black.

your long and_____ hair

6.

My hair is short and brown.

your short and

_____ _____

7.

My hair is straight and blonde.

your _____ and _____ hair

8.

My hair is curly and brown.

your _____ and brown _____

A GAME 玩遊戲

⭐ 先把下面的棋盤填上你喜歡的顏色，然後邀請朋友一起來玩這個遊戲。準備一顆骰子，骰子面上的六個點，分別代表1、2、3、4、5、6。二人輪流擲骰子，按照骰子面上所顯示的數字，從START開始前進，如果走到有圖案的格子時，就按照圖案內容做出相應的動作。誰最先回到START，誰就獲勝。

ANSWERS 答案

TEST 小測驗

1. head   face   eye(s)   nose   mouth
   tongue   tooth / teeth   ear(s)   cheek(s)   hair

3. (a) my arm / my arms   (b) my body   (c) my hand / my hands
   (d) my foot / my feet   (e) my leg / my legs

4. (a) My hair is blonde.
   (b) My hair is black.
   (c) My hair is long.
   (d) My hair is short.

EXERCISE BOOK 練習冊

P.1-2
略

P.3-4
略

P.5-6
填色：略
1. red   2. brown   3. hair   4. blonde   5. black
6. brown hair   7. straight, blonde   8. curly, hair